Rory Branagan (Detective)
The Den of Danger

by Andrew Clover
and Ralph Lazar

RORY
BRANAGAN

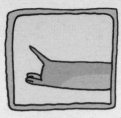

WILKINS

WELKIN

CASSIDY
CALLAGHAN

MRS WELKIN

SEAMUS
BRANAGAN

STEPHEN MAYSMITH

JACK
'MUSCLE'
THOMPSON

JULIA

PADDER
BRANAGAN

DEREK
'DENT-HEAD'
O'MALLEY

BIN BOY

GUY
'THE EYES'
MURPHY

MICHAEL
MULLIGAN

MARK
'THE GENIUS'
O'GATISS

THE SHEEP

THE BEAR

THE HAMSTER

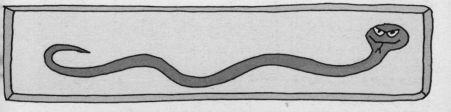

BLACK MAMBA

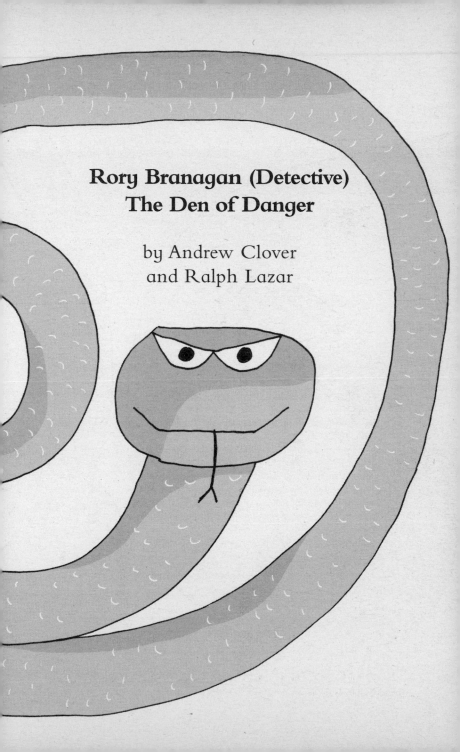

Rory Branagan (Detective)
The Den of Danger

by Andrew Clover
and Ralph Lazar

First published in Great Britain by
HarperCollins *Children's Books* in 2020
HarperCollins *Children's Book*s is a division of HarperCollins*Publishers* Ltd,
HarperCollins Publishers
1 London Bridge Street
London SE1 9GF

The HarperCollins website address is
www.harpercollins.co.uk
1

ISBN 978–0–00–826598–4

Andrew Clover and Ralph Lazar assert the moral right to be identified as
the author and illustrator of the work respectively.
A CIP catalogue record for this title is available from the British Library.

Printed and bound in England by CPI Group (UK) Ltd, Croydon, CR0 4YY

Dedicated to *Roald Dahl, Enid Blyton, Raymond Chandler, Charles Dickens, P. G. Wodehouse, Dorothy Parker, Jonathan Swift, Jane Austen, William Shakespeare* – and all writers who now **read** in the great treehouse in the sky.

What I LOVE about being a detective is . . .

. . . if you're going somewhere
that seems normal and boring, if you
EXPLORE . . .

. . . you find it has secrets and *doors to strange gardens* and **MYSTERIES**.

3

And sometimes the **MYSTERIES** just seem *too* BIG and too *CONFUSING* . . .

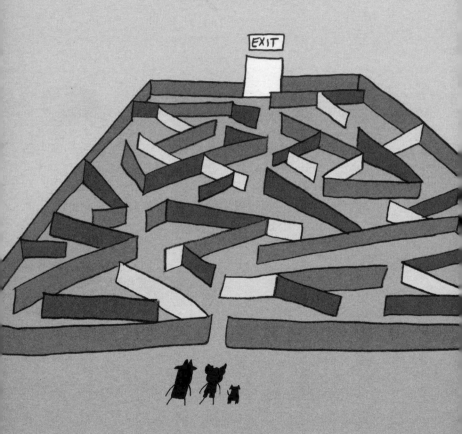

But if you *look at things from another angle,* you find . . .

... there's ALWAYS a way through!

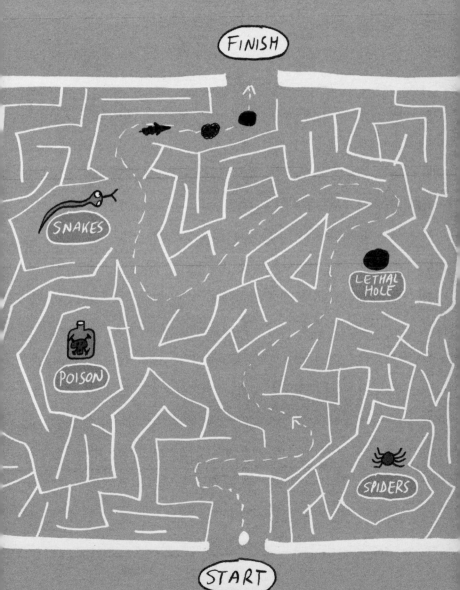

And even if you find yourself in a *Place of DEADLY DANGER* (being chased down dark corridors by *bad guys* and *lethal creatures*) . . .

. . . if you *keep cool* and *keep **searching,*** you find ***the Place of DEADLY DANGER*** might also be . . .

(I *LOVE* that about detectiving!)
But in this story I find sometimes the
places you must investigate can be . . .

. . . inside your own head.

And you can't always run from the bad guys, because the bad guys are *inside your head.*

BUT I *also* find that inside your head might be the *person you've looked for all your life* – and for me that's my dad.

In this story, I find where he's gone. **BUT** (and it's a big but) I do also find myself . . .

. . . *stuck* in the DEADLIEST OF DEADLY DANGERS with BAD GUYS and *LETHAL CREATURES* – and they are NOT *just in my head.* They are **right in front of me**, *biting with their sharp, poisonous teeth!!*

CHAPTER ONE:
News of a CRIME

It doesn't start in deadly danger. *As it all starts*, I am just hanging out in the front garden in the warm sun.

Cat is texting.

Wilkins is weeing on gate posts.

Wilkins thinks if a house smells of his wee, then it's his. Wilkins even thinks if he weed on *Buckingham Palace* . . .

. . . it would become his.

Wilkins weeing on the palace

Wilkins weeing on corgis

He thinks if he weed on the queen's corgis, they'd become his army. Then he'd *wee* on the throne, the crown *and the queen*, and become *king* of his own wee-smelling kingdom.

Wilkins weeing on the queen

Wilkins on the throne, king of his wee-smelling kingdom

I'm just looking at snails. I have one
that is racing towards me at *top speed*.

It's as if he thinks I am God of All
Snails.

'Rory,' says Cat, 'we need to go over the
facts of the case.'

'What case?' I say.

I now touch the snail. He thinks the God of All Snails has turned *evil*, and he's *under attack*. He's **retreating**.

'**THE case**,' says Cat. '*You know* . . . seven years ago, your dad *mysteriously disappeared* . . . I have been helping you find him. What have we *found out?*'

'We know he's *hiding* in the place he was once happiest,' I say. (The snail has gone into his shell now.) 'We know that because of the secret letter.'

'We *also* know he was World Rally Champion,' Cat says.

'He was also a stunt driver for Daredevil Motors, and he made a festival called Car Bonanza that he sold to Michael Mulligan, the scariest *crime lord* in the world.'

'Ah, Mulligan's not so bad,' I say.
'When I met him at Car Bonanza he told
me he was Dad's friend.'

I have a very *juicy* leaf, and I'm trying
to tempt the snail back out again.

Suddenly Cat loses it.

'RORY!' she says. 'Are you going to FOCUS, or are you going to *daydream like an eejit and play with snails?*'

'Snails are important,' I tell her.

'We also know,' she snarls, 'on the last day you saw him, your dad LEFT YOU IN A CAR and *RAN OFF!*'

Suddenly I am *remembering* Dad parking his car by the old church and LEAVING me.

Cat has made me UPSET, and I have a lump in my throat.

'WHICH *DIRECTION* did your dad run off in?' asks Cat.

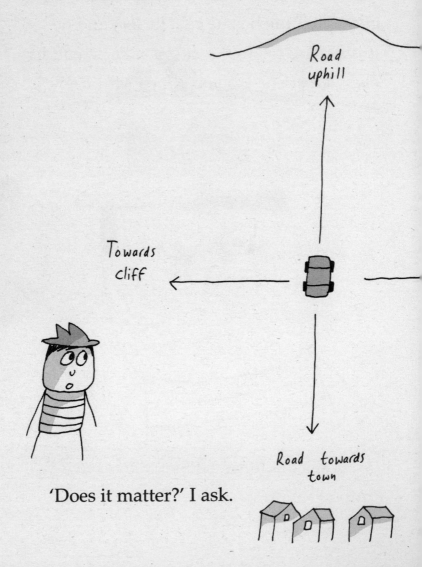

Road uphill

Towards cliff

Road towards town

'Does it matter?' I ask.

'We know the police were looking for him. We know they've been looking *ever since*. My hunch is he ran, he *hid*, and he **stayed hidden**. So the *direction* he ran off in – *yes, it matters*! Do you REMEMBER?'

Church

I *try* to remember. I try to picture Dad.
In my mind his face is all *shimmering*, like
a magic person. (That's the trouble with
stuff in my head: I'm never sure it's *real*.)

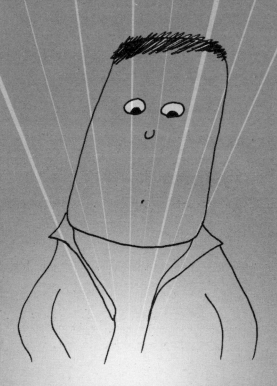

'I don't *remember*!' I complain. 'It was
too long ago! I was only three!'

Just then Wilkins starts growling. He's *looking* across the street.

It makes me think of our last case, when Wilkins suspected the bad guy from the first. If I'd paid attention to him, I might have rescued my Uncle Kenny before he was *crushed by a car*, and ended up in hospital. I definitely pay attention now.

Wilkins is looking at the house of the *Gilligans*. The dad is called 'Guinea Pig' Gilligan because they have forty-three guinea pigs. He's recently back from hospital.

He was *poisoned* by a woman who rented a room in our attic, under the orders of a *gangster* called *Jack 'Muscle' Thompson*.

I'm friends with Guinea Pig's son.

We call him *Corner Boy*, because he's always standing on the street corner, looking *fierce*. But right now, he's crouching in Mrs Welkin's garden, *peeking* at two men.

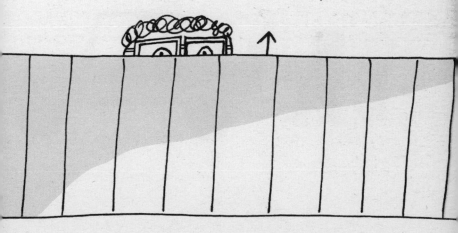

They're carrying big boxes towards a huge black jeep.

Now *my* eyes are peering out *all eager* like a snail's. I have *seen* that car. (*But WHERE?*) And I think I hear *squeaking*. (But **WHY?**)

'What do you think is happening over there?' I ask Cat.

But she's not even looking. She's
peering at a newspaper on the pavement.
She bends down and picks it up.

The men put their boxes in the boot.
They drive off.

'*Corner Boy!*' I shout, running over.
'What was in those boxes?'

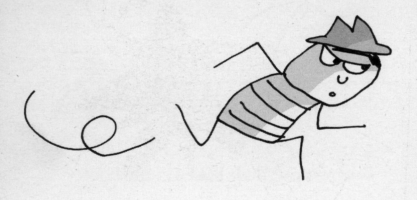

Corner Boy stands up and . . .

. . . punches me in the face.

Luckily I *expected it*. (I know Corner Boy does this!)

I duck. I catch his fist, swing him round, JUDO his leg and pin him down.

'*What was in those boxes?*' I repeat.

'*Nothing!*' he says, but his voice goes *squeaky*.

'Was it *guinea pigs*?'

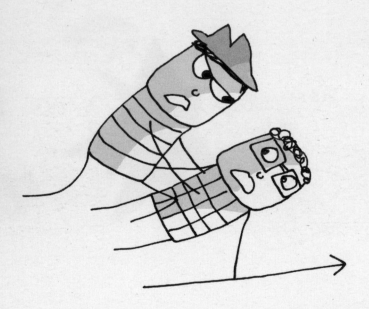

'NO!' He scrambles to his feet and runs into the house. *Why is he running off when I'm asking questions?*

Cat waves the newspaper.

'Rory! Come here. We need to talk about this!'

'You, come *here*,' I command. 'We need to talk about THIS!'

But she doesn't even listen! She heads into my house as if she's now weed on it and it's *hers*. Furious, I follow.

'Rory,' she says as I find her in my front room, 'I have discovered something *important* about your dad.'

That gets my attention. She now shows me the paper.

'DIAMONDS FOUND,'

says the front page.

'"Diamonds have been found,"' she reads, '"that have been traced to the Great Diamond Heist of 2013, in which four men stole the Dame Norton Diamond, the most expensive jewel ever stolen."'

'What has *this* got to do with my dad?' I say.

'"A man *died* that day,"' Cat reads, '"a known criminal called Mark 'The Genius' O'Gatiss. His body was found in the yard of the old Anderson factory, showing traces of snake venom."'

'WHAT HAS THIS GOT TO DO WITH MY DAD?' I repeat.

'"The getaway driver is known to have been former World Rally Champion, Padder Branagan. His three-year-old son was found in the vehicle. Branagan has been missing ever since that day – as has the Dame Norton Diamond. No one has ever been convicted of the theft, or the killing."'

And there's a picture of Dad.

CHAPTER TWO:
A Big, Useless Dingbat

I am so surprised I almost faint.

Suddenly . . . Wilkins starts *barking*. I
think there's someone coming towards
our house. (Somehow he always knows!) I
go to the corridor.

Immediately my brother's BIG
HEAD appears from the kitchen.

'Er, EXCUSE ME,'
he says, 'SOME OF US
ARE ACTUALLY TRYING
TO DO SOME HOMEWORK!

He's got his girlfriend round – *Julia*. He *says* he's doing homework. But whenever I've peeked, they've just been writing love notes, and eating hummus.

My brother is SOOOOO annoying.

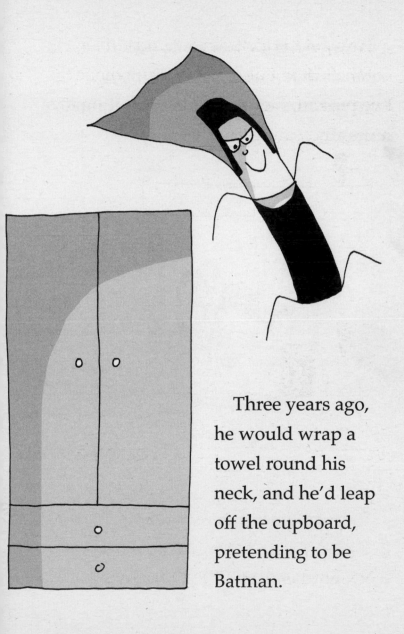

Three years ago, he would wrap a towel round his neck, and he'd leap off the cupboard, pretending to be Batman.

Now he thinks he's some sort of sophisticated European *ladies' man*, who sits around in town centres, eating hummus.

He's got the hummus pot now. I want to **SpLAT** it on his big head. But I don't. (*Give me credit. I don't!*)

'And some of US,' I tell him, 'are actually doing DETECTIVE work!'

'You're not a detective,' he scoffs, 'you're a DINGBAT!'

There IS a knock at the door now. (Wilkins is always right!) I answer it and find . . .

Michael Mulligan, the crime lord.

Normally I'd be TERRIFIED to find a GANGSTER at my front door. But now I am *delighted*.

'*SEE!*' I want to shout to my brother. 'I AM a detective, and I have a real, actual CRIMINAL right HERE!' And I want to slap my bottom right in my brother's face

– slap,

slap,

slap!

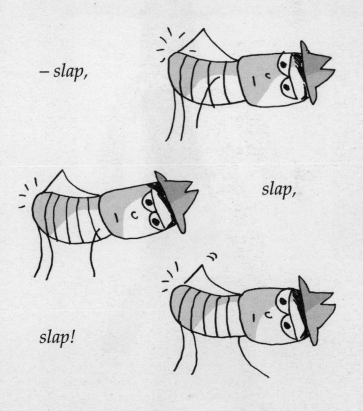

But I *don't*. (*Give me credit, I don't!*)

'Mr Mulligan,' I just say, 'how can I help you?'

And he steps into the house.

'I have just come from seeing your Uncle Kenny in hospital,' he rumbles.

'He'll be there a few days yet, but he'll *recover*. And it's thanks to you, Rory, that the woman who tried to kill him was caught. This is to thank you, on behalf of the Car Bonanza festival.' He pulls out a giant gun made from chocolate.

'Thank you,' I tell him. 'Would you like some?'

'I'm on a diet,' he says. 'No meat, dairy or sugar.'

I unwrap the trigger and eat some.

Cat hasn't even come out of the front room. I have noticed this before. She's SCARED of Michael Mulligan. I am *not*. I am thinking this is a perfect chance to learn *information*.

'Did you read about the Great Diamond Heist in the paper?' I ask.

'I knew O'Gatiss,' he says. 'A BRILLIANT man – clever, kind, *smart*. If I find *anyone* who had *anything* to do with his death, I'll visit their home with a steam roller.'

He looks into my eyes.

'I believe *you* were there that day. Do you remember *anyone* who was in that car with you?'

Suddenly I see O'Gatiss in my head, but his eyes are wild and scary and for a moment I'm too terrified to think.

But then I do. I think back to the day . . .

All I *remember* for sure is I had an ice cream, we drove very fast, and I felt sick. I don't want to tell Mulligan that.

'I don't remember!' I tell him.

'If you remember *anything*, call me,' he says, and he hands me a card.

'I will!'

'Good man!' says Mulligan, and he leaves.

As I walk him out to his Rolls-Royce,
I'm wanting to ask if he knows anything
about the black jeep.

But then O'Gatiss swoops into my head,
eyes wild, like a big bat. I'm scared. I am
now wanting to go back inside and cuddle
Wilkins.

But the TERRORS of the day are only getting STARTED. Because just then I turn, I see the sun gleaming on the wet tarmac of our road, and an ENORMOUS shape appears.

Is it a Zeppelin that's crash-landed?
Is it a zombie elephant?
No, it's . . .

. . . Stephen Maysmith, police detective!!

'*Young man,*' he calls. 'Would you care to come to the station to answer some questions about the disappearance of your dad?'

'I'd be happy to!' I tell him. I would walk to Timbuktu if that would help find Dad.

'I'll drive you in my car,' says Maysmith.

Even *better*! I LOVE going in the police car! I run in and tell Mrs Welkin.

She is a neighbour who looks after us when Mum's away. She's in the kitchen with Wilkins. She wants to come. Wilkins wants to come.

Two minutes later, we're off.

CHAPTER THREE:
The Police Station

The police station is actually BRILLIANT.
It's just like on TV . . .

We go to a special room, with big glass windows that you can't see through.

I think of that Bond film, where the baddie lives by a big tank of sharks.

I am thinking all the policemen out there are actually sharks, except they're swimming around eating doughnuts and filling out forms.

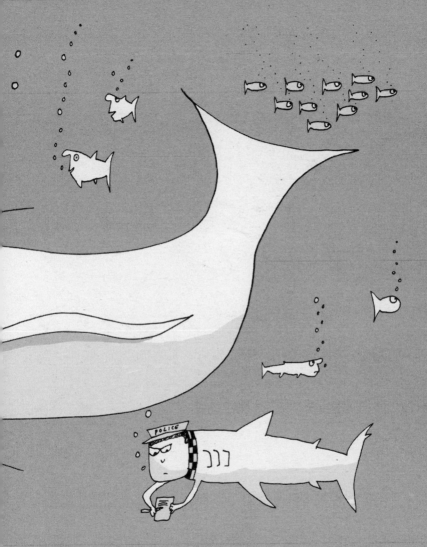

Except, that is, for Stephen Maysmith,
who's a big fat whale.

He now comes in with a tape recorder and some custard creams. He offers one to me. He eats four himself.

'Your dad was last seen,' he says, 'on July the fourth, 2013, at eleven thirty-one am. I myself took a picture of him.'

He lays out the picture.

It shows Dad in an old
am in the back seat, unde
blanket. I've never seen t

'I had no reason to arrest him at that
time,' Maysmith tells me. 'We *now* know
he'd been involved in the theft of the
Dame Norton Diamond.'

ow . . . I know this has been in
he paper, but it still ANNOYS me to
have Maysmith *accusing Dad of being a
criminal.* 'I do not BELIEVE Dad was
involved in a CRIME,' I tell him.

'I'm afraid he is our principal suspect,'
he says.

What?! '*WHY?*'

'Well, he's *disappeared* . . . and so has the
diamond.'

I am now wanting to smash Maysmith's biscuits on his head.

'Just tell me the FACTS you know,' I say (icily).

He lays out a diagram, filled with facts. He reads them out.

The Events of July 4th 2013

11.12 – A black van parks outside McAlister's Jeweller's and Muscle's Pets.

11.13 – Three men enter Muscle's Pets.

11.15 – First explosion in basement of Muscle's Pets. Leonard McAlister calls police. Forty officers begin hurrying towards the scene.

11.16 – Second explosion. Three men enter McAlister's Jeweller's through hole in basement, knock out McAlister.

11.24 – Arrival of Padder Branagan in blue sports car.

'It doesn't make sense!' I tell him. 'If the baddies already have a black Ford van, why would they need another driver?'

'We know the driver of the black Ford van took a call at eleven twenty. We believe the caller was your dad, *threatening* him. The driver then drove off, FAST.'

'Why don't you *find* the driver and interview him?' I ask.

'We don't know who he was! He was wearing a mask!'

'What sort of mask?'

'A chicken mask!'

'A *chicken*??!!'

Maysmith carries on reading . . .

11.25 – Padder Branagan enters Muscle's Pets.

11.26 – Four men (including Branagan) leave Muscle's Pets.

11.27 – Blue Audi drives off.

11.41 – Mark 'The Genius' O'Gatiss is found dead in the yard of the old Anderson factory.

'How did O'Gatiss die?' I ask.

'We believe it was *murder* by snake bite.'

That sounds like rubbish. 'What *evidence* do you have?' I ask.

'There were signs of a scuffle in the yard.

Footprints. A torn button. Part of a bookmark . . . There were pinpricks on his back. There were also poisons in his system: *dendrotoxins* and *three-finger toxins.'*

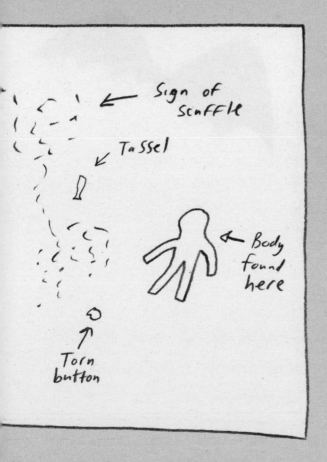

Sign of scuffle

Tassel

Body found here

Torn button

Suddenly a BIG DETECTIVE THOUGHT comes swooping into my head like a bat.

'Did you say POISON?' I ask. 'Doesn't *that* suggest the involvement of Jack "Muscle" Thompson?'

'We thought that!' Maysmith fires back.
'Muscle owned the pet shop next door,
where *listening equipment* was found!'

'REALLY???!!!' I say. 'So there IS
evidence he was involved!'

'The pet shop *was* called Muscle's Pets!'
says Maysmith (quite *patronisingly*).

That annoys me again.

'We believed Muscle had heard about the Dame Norton Diamond,' says Maysmith, 'and planned the heist . . .'
'That sounds LIKELY!' I say.

GROUND FLOOR

Muscle's Pets

Office

Shop floor

McAlister's Jeweller's

Office

Shop floor

Street

'But we interrogated Muscle,' says Maysmith. 'We couldn't prove he *STOLE* anything, or *KILLED* anyone. We couldn't find a murder weapon or a witness!!'

BASEMENT LEVEL

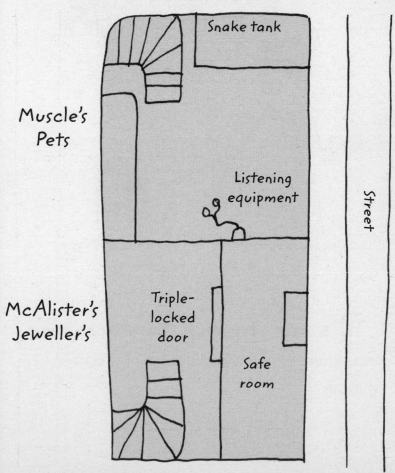

'Do you believe he's innocent?'

'NO!' says Maysmith. 'But we need *new* evidence – a *murder* weapon, a credible *witness* . . .'

'I just don't get it!' I say. 'You say FORTY police officers were coming . . .'

'Yes, they were!'

He shows me a map of the town centre.

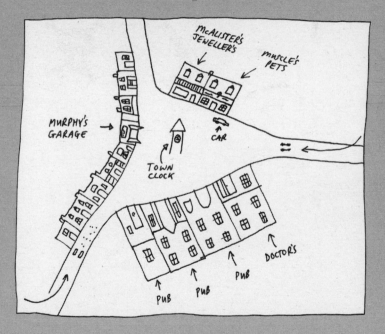

'Four police cars coming here,' he says. 'Two police bikes coming here. Ten police officers and two police horses coming here . . .'

'*So HOW did the baddies get away?*'

'Somehow they caused a power cut.
Some CCTV cameras kept working – the
ones with batteries. Most didn't.'

'This is a CCTV image of your dad's car outside the jeweller's at eleven twenty-six,' says Maysmith, and he produces a picture.

'This is the same scene at eleven twenty-eight, only two minutes later.' He lays down a nearly identical picture.

But I am a World Master of Spot the Difference. There is one obvious change: the car has gone. But then I notice one other thing.

'In the second picture,' I say, '*windows* are open at the back of Murphy's garage.'

'What does that suggest?' Maysmith asks.

'Maybe the car flew through the window and opened them!'

'Do you *remember* this?' he persists.

'No!'

Suddenly Maysmith LOSES it.

'I have had ENOUGH of your CHILDISH THEORIES!!'

'Mr *Maysmith*!' snaps Mrs Welkin, as if she's about to put the big man over her knee and give him a slap.

Maysmith recovers. He now passes over a picture of a man. He has frizzy hair, tasselled loafers, a tracksuit and a cravat.

'This is Jack "Muscle" Thompson,' says Maysmith. 'Did you see him in the car that day?'

'No!'

'And this is Mark "The Genius" O'Gatiss . . .' says Maysmith, showing me another picture.

And suddenly, like when I first saw his picture in the newspaper, memories *are* coming back!

'I DO remember him!' I say.

Maysmith is excited.

'What *do* you remember?' he says.

'I think . . .'

'*Yes?*'

'I *remember* . . .'

'YES?'

'He gave me a kitten.'

'A *kitten?*'

I am remembering now. I LIKED that kitten!

'But there's something I don't *understand*,' I say. 'You know all the *timings* and *arrivals* of the criminals . . .'

'We have most of it on CCTV!'

'So HOW COME you didn't see the *faces* of the three men?'

'Because they were ALL wearing MASKS!'

He slams down a picture.

The three men DO have masks. One's a bear, one's a hamster, the other's a sheep.

And suddenly I REMEMBER this! The baddies WERE wearing masks! I didn't think that was so weird at the time. I was three. I often wore a mask myself. I once spent a whole day as a duck.

'Mr Hamster was the one who died!' says Maysmith. 'That was O'Gatiss. The mask was found by his body. We *suspect* Muscle Thompson was Mr Sheep.'

'So who was the bear?'
'We don't *know*!' says Maysmith.

'You need to find that bear,' I tell him.
'Find that bear and you'll find the diamond!'

'WE ARE TRYING TO FIND THAT BEAR!'
bellows Maysmith.

'I think I should get Rory home now,'
says Mrs Welkin.

CHAPTER FOUR:
The Storm Starts

And ten minutes later, I'm home. I go straight round to see Cat Callaghan, who is busy learning about snakes on her dad's computer. I tell her everything I remember – the timings, the kitten, Muscle's Pets . . .

She listens *very* carefully, then . . .

'So the three masked men entered the
jeweller's at *eleven sixteen*,' she says. 'But
they didn't LEAVE for TEN minutes, and
then, *only after your dad came in.*'

'Yes . . . Does that suggest something?'

'It suggests the men needed help because something was *stopping* them leaving. What *could* that be?'

I'm trying to imagine, but I can't work it out.

'Are you *sure* you can't remember who was in the car that day?' Cat asks.

I TRY to remember. I think of the picture of Jack 'Muscle' Thompson. I think of his cravat, his tracksuit, his brown tasselled shoes . . .

I get a brainwave . . .

'*I saw Muscle Thompson's shoes!*' I say.

'WHAT? In the getaway car?'

'No, TODAY! The man who was taking boxes from Corner Boy's house!' I say.

'WHAT?'

'We *know* Muscle Thompson knows the Gilligans! He made that woman *poison* Corner Boy's dad!'

'And what do you *think* was in those boxes?'

'I *think* they were filled with *guinea pigs*!'

And it's as if we're in a Horror Film about Guinea Pigs. Suddenly there's a loud RUMBLE of thunder outside.

KERRRASSH!

'And if that was Muscle Thompson,' I say, 'we need to stop him – before he does something to those guinea pigs!'

KERAKKAKUMBLE!!

LIGHTNING now fills the sky.

'But, Rory, how do we know where he has taken them?'

'*I recognised that black jeep*. I know where to find it!'

'WHERE?'

'It's always parked near school! On Niall Horan Drive!'

'Well, LET'S GO THERE NOW!'

I'm a bit scared our mums will try to stop us. So we leave by the garden wall.

'It looks like an EVIL STORM is coming!' says Cat.

'I am a detective,' I tell her. 'I'm not scared of a bit of weather!'

KERAK-KA-KA-KERBANG!!

'You sure?' says Cat.

'It wouldn't matter if it was the *worst storm* of all time!' I say. 'We *have* to rescue those guinea pigs!'

KERA-KACKA-
KACKA-
BOOM!!

A mighty lightning flash
STRIKES the land!

Two minutes later, we're turning into Niall Horan Drive. And I was right about this. The house we want is Number 666. I can see the black jeep.

CHAPTER FIVE:
The Den of Danger

'Hmmm,' says Cat. 'So either this house belongs to Muscle Thompson . . . or the owner's been watching a TV show called *Make Your House Look Like a Criminal's*!'

'What makes this house look like a criminal's?'

'Em,' she says. 'Let's see: the CCTV, the three-metre-high barbed-wire-topped electric fence, the signs saying **"BEWARE OF THE DOG"** …'

'. . . All that leads to an *impression!*'

Just then a squirrel jumps off a tree on to the wire.

BANG!

It falls off.

I look at the back of the car.

'Those boxes are still in there!' I say.

'Those guinea pigs must be TERRIFIED!'

'So how are we going to get to them?'
says Cat.

I think.

'Well, if we had some *drones*,' I tell her, 'then they could fly us up over the gate.'

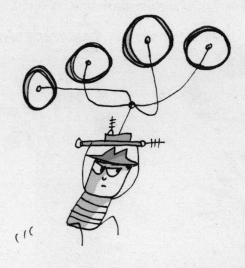

'But where would we find some drones?' she says. 'And just say Muscle saw us?'

'So it would be better,' I say, 'if we were hidden *inside* something – like some *trees*!'

'But if Muscle sees some trees flying over the fence,' says Cat, 'he won't say,

"Fair enough – some flying trees!" He'll get a *BAZOOKA* and start BLASTING!'

I am getting *annoyed*. I am the one who's having ideas. She is just shooting them down in flames.

'How do *you* reckon we get in?' I ask.
Just then two men come out of the
house. I only really see the first one. He is
a skinny youth with mad eyes. He looks
the sort who'd torture cats for fun.

'Get down,' says Cat.

Crouching behind the brick wall, we hear a man with a London accent saying: 'Put out those bins. The bin men will be here any sec.'

We are behind the gate as the skinny
boy pushes the bin out. It's a black one.

Thirty seconds later, he's back with a
green bin. He returns to the house without
noticing us.

Cat has the sneakiest, *catty* look on her face.

'And *that*, my friend, is *how we'll get in,*' she says. 'As soon as the bins are emptied, we will climb in. We will then be *wheeled into the compound*. We'll go to that car and rescue those guinea pigs.'

KERSPLASHAPACK!

With the words 'guinea pigs', lightning
strikes, wind *howls* and rain *lashes* down.
'I am not staying here,' I tell her,
'waiting for some *bins* to be emptied!'

'The park is just round the corner,' says
Cat. 'Let's walk there and get out of the
rain.'

CHAPTER SIX:
The Park

And I am happy with that. If it meant I
didn't have to climb into some bins that
could belong to Muscle Thompson, I
would gladly walk to every park in the
world. I would do . . .

Rory Branagan's Great Park Challenge

(in which I walk to every park there is)

Bruichladdich
Bottomical Garden
(lots of bottoms)

Buncrana Botanical
Garden (lots of plants)

Ballymena Park
(with woods)

START

Jason Byrne
Badger Park
(bring a
badger)

FINISH

Dara O'Brien Dog Park
(you can bring a dog)

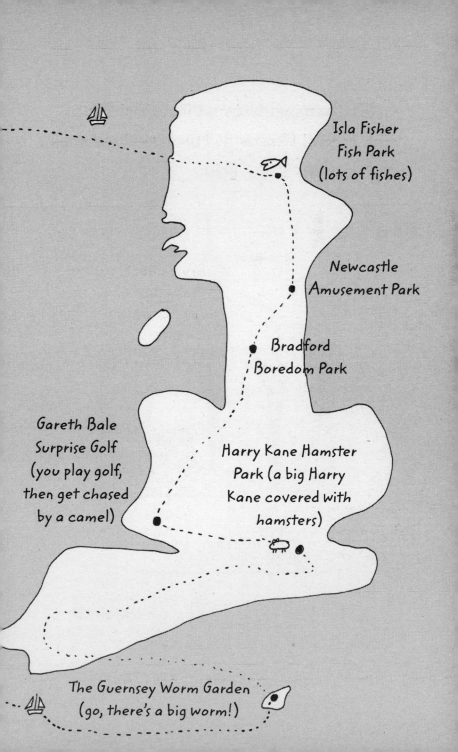

Five minutes later, we're under the
bandstand. I know it. This is where I was,
that last day I saw Dad.

As the rain *batters* down on the duck
pond, the *memories* flood back . . .

It was HOT that day. Dad bought me a
DOUBLE-CHOCOLATE ICE CREAM.

It was the first time I saw Wilkins. He
was *sooo* small and *sooooo* long.

As he charged around, he was like one of those long balloons, losing air.

He chased ducks.

He had a fight with a much bigger dog.

He chased a Frisbee.

He jumped on to a chair,
then on to a table.

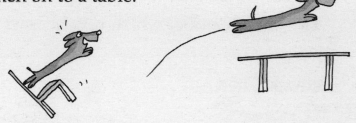

As he flew by, he knocked my ice
cream. I didn't care.

As he walked home with Mrs Welkin,
he chewed my ice-cream cone. It looked
like a cigar.

'I'm remembering *loads* about the last time I saw Dad,' I tell Cat.

'Do you remember which way he *went* yet?' says Cat.

I think. Then . . .

'I actually remember him getting a phone call!' I say. 'He was *right there* by the pond!'

'Who was it?' says Cat.
'I don't know . . . but he seemed *surprised*. He seemed *annoyed* . . .'

'Maybe it was the bad guys, asking him to join the heist!' says Cat.

'And I don't believe he was *meant* to be anything to do with it. If he was planning on joining, why would he bring a toddler?' I said.

'I remember he put me on his
shoulders, and he took me to the car . . .'

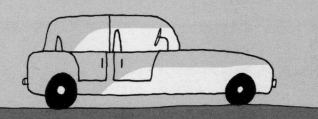

'It was our *blue* car, the one from the
CCTV! *Not* the one in Stephen Maysmith's
last picture of Dad.'

'*Interesting!*' says Cat. Then . . . 'But those guinea pigs are waiting.'

I suddenly think of those guinea pigs, all hidden in boxes in the car. They won't understand about the lightning and thunder. They'll be fearing there are big EAGLES out there, with bombs.

'We'd better go back,' says Cat, 'and see if the bins have been emptied.'

We sneak back to the
house and peek round
an alleyway.

We see that, unfortunately, the
have been emptied.

I open the green one. It smells like compost and cat sick.

'I'll take the black,' I say.

I open it, and

jump

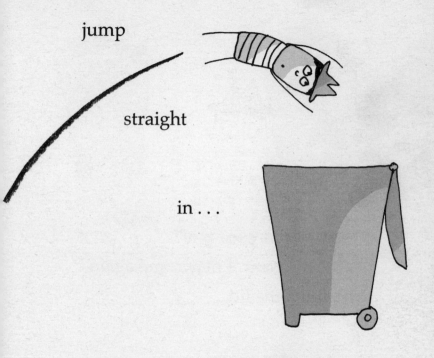

straight

in . . .

. . . before seeing my mistake.

It stinks of egg and used nappy. But
I close the lid. As I do, I can hear Cat
leaping into the green bin.

'Cat,' I say. I open my lid.
'What?' She opens hers.

'How is it in your bin?'
'Most pleasant. I may come again.'
She shuts the lid.

'Cat?'

'*What?*' She opens the lid.

'There are holes in the side of them. I think they're bullet holes.'

'Convenient,' she says. 'We can look out.'

I look out.

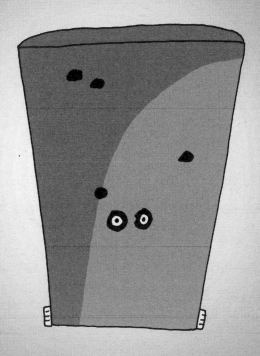

Just then I see the kid with the mad eyes. I shut my lid fast. He now walks towards the bin and starts wheeling me.

As he does, I am thinking: *Oh my God, I soooooooooo hope he doesn't look inside, or notice this bin is heavy.*

But he doesn't. He wheels me into the compound. He goes back for Cat.

As he does, I see an upstairs window open. I hear a cockney voice saying: 'Those bins'll get blown over. Put 'em in the garage.'

Of course now I want to open my lid and say: 'Don't put us in the garage, we just want to go to the car and rescue those guinea pigs!!!'

But I don't. Because I'm not NUTS.

I just lie bunched at the bottom of the bin like a used nappy as I'm wheeled *into* the garage.

I'm now terrified. I stay still as the boy goes back for Cat. He brings her in and then shuts the door.

I stay still as death as Cat . . . leaps from her bin. She inspects the garage.

'Rory,' she whispers, opening my lid. 'Bad news . . . He *locked the garage door.*'

Oh NO! I feel like those guinea pigs. I feel we're TRAPPED, and we'll never escape! I am so scared I feel sick.

'Get out of that bin,' Cat says.

I do. She now sneaks to the door that leads into the house. This one isn't locked. She peeks round it.

'What can you see?' I whisper, so quietly.

'The front door's to the right. A hallway to the left. I can see stairs, and a door with frosted glass that leads to a lounge. I can see a *huge* yellow dog in there. He looks like a *lion*!'

I'm trying to picture it all.

'If we go to the front door,' Cat whispers, 'the dog could *see* us before we're out.'

NO!

'It might be safer to go across the hall and up the stairs,' she says. 'And try to escape through a window.'

I am boiling with fear and confusion.

'Plus . . . who knows what we might find up there?' she says, grinning. She's like this. When we're in danger, she *grins*.

I don't. I say nothing. I do nothing.

'You stay here if you like,' she says. 'I'm going for the stairs.' And she GOES.

Oh God, she's GONE! I want to be LEFT ALL ALONE even less than I want to be found by that dog.

I now count

1,

2,

3,

and . . .

CHAPTER SEVEN:
Another Level of Fear

Heart beating, holding my breath . . .
I now DART into the hallway.

I see the dog. *Does he hear me? Does he smell me?*

He doesn't move. I tiptoe to the stairs.

Cat's waiting at
the top. She smiles.

'Deadly Branagan,' she
mouths, 'follow me!'
She leaps like a rabbit
into the room on her left.
I follow. She shuts
the door behind us.

It's an office room. There are shelves on one side, and one of them gets my interest: it has a tank on it with a snail inside!

Cat's face breaks into a slow, sly smile. I say, '*What?*'

'This must be the room that the-man-
who-might-be-Muscle-Thompson was in,
when he was yelling commands about the
bins. Think back . . .'

I think back to the man at the window.

'What did you *notice*?' she asks.

'I noticed a cactus beside him,' I say. 'What did *you* notice?'

'I saw *two* windows from outside. I can only see *one* in here. And there was only *one* door in the corridor!'

'So?'

'I think,' she says, eyes *twinkling*,
'there's a SECRET ROOM, and I'm
thinking we should INVESTIGATE!'

I'm suddenly thinking we have
stumbled on something that's BIGGER
than just guinea pigs.

'But how would we get in?' I ask.

Cat goes to the shelves. She tries to pull them. She presses buttons. She pulls drawers. She finds remote controls. But nothing happens.

Meanwhile, I pull the snail out of its tank.

But it's not a real snail. It has a button
on the side of it, which I press.

And that's when the entire shelf *spins
round*.

'Oh my God!' says Cat.

'I told you,' I say. 'Snails are *important*.'

We nip into the secret room to find
it's *completely filled* with brightly lit glass
tanks. Some have water, some don't. I see
bubbles and pondweed. I see jellyfish. I
see scorpionfish. I see a scorpion.

Cat peers into a tank. '*Ah!*'

'What?'

She finds a weird pole. It has a sort of
huge peg on the end. She reaches it into
a tank.

'*What are you doing?*' I ask.

'This!' she says.

And she lifts out a snake!!!

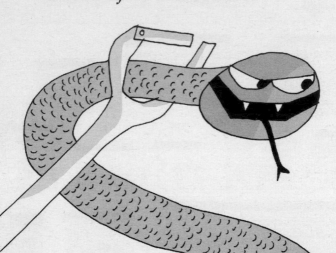

The peg is holding its head. She grips its tail in the other hand.

'You just have to keep the head away from yourself,' she says, 'and you're fine!'

I say nothing. I'm so scared I may never speak again.

'I'd say this is why he wanted the guinea pigs,' says Cat. 'To feed this lot.'

I am thinking of the guinea pigs being fed to a snake.

'Hold the pole,' says Cat.
I do.
'Hold out your left hand.'
I do. I don't know why, but I do.

And suddenly I'm holding the snake!!!!!!

I am so scared my heart could leap from my mouth and be gulped down by the snake.

'Cat,' I whimper quietly, *'why am I holding a snake?'*

'Look at this collection!' she says.
'That's a python,

that's an anaconda,

that's a corn snake . . .

What do you notice?'
    '*Snakes*?' I squeak.
    'And none of them are venomous . . .'

'. . . except *that* one,' she says, pointing to the creature I'm holding. 'The black mamba, the most *deadly snake in the world.*'

'But this snake is *grey*!' I whimper, so hoping she's wrong.

'The black mamba *is* grey,' she replies. 'It's the *inside* of its mouth that's *black*!'

Just then the snake turns his coffin-shaped head.

He opens his mouth and goes:

'CCCCCCCCC.'

The inside of his mouth is *jet black*!

Cat is now looking behind the snake's tank. '*Ha!*' she says.

What now?

'Snake bite *antivenom*!' she explains, showing me some syringes. 'Very *valuable*! To make this, you need to *milk* the snakes for poison!'

'I'm keeping those!' she says.

She puts them in her pocket.

Just then we hear a noise.

'IS THERE SOMEONE
UP THERE?'

calls a cockney voice.

Oh NO!

Cat pulls out her phone and texts fast.
'Who are you texting?'

'Stephen Maysmith,' she whispers.
'Giving this address. We need help!'

But just then . . .

A man comes in. He's wearing tasselled loafers. His dead-lizard eyes turn and stare right at me.

'Are you Jack "Muscle" Thompson?'
I ask.

CHAPTER EIGHT:
Jack 'Muscle' Thompson

'What are you doing in my house?' says Muscle. He looks at Cat. 'And WHAT are YOU . . .'

'We're the ones holding the black mamba,' Cat tells him. 'We will ask the questions.'

His eyes gleam.

'Is it true you tried to have Guinea Pig Gilligan killed?' I ask him.

He says nothing. But sometimes it's what people DON'T say that counts. He doesn't say, 'Who's Guinea Pig Gilligan?'

'Do you deny it?' I ask.

'I deny *everything*,' he says. 'But I would say the man was a thief. He's had his warning: *don't steal round here.*'

'So you're letting him off?' says Cat. 'Just forcing him to give you his guinea pigs, to feed to your snakes.'

Muscle's eyes widen.

'How do you know that?' he says.

'We know EVERYTHING,' I tell him. 'We are detectives.'

'Are you Rory Branagan?' asks Muscle.

'YES!' I tell him.

'And we think *you* killed Mark "The Genius" O'Gatiss!' snarls Cat.

Muscle turns to her. His lizard eyes betray NOTHING.

'The police *questioned* me about that,' he says. 'They found *no evidence*.'

I'm thinking: *But what would the police do
if they found out you have a black mamba?*

'What do you actually *want*?' Muscle
asks, looking at me.

'I just want to find my dad,' I tell him.

'He's trying to remember which way his dad went that day!' says Cat.

Muscle smiles. It's a big, ugly one – the grin of a snake.

'But that's exactly what *I* want too!' he says.

'WHY?' I shoot back.

'Maybe I've just been reading about it all in the paper,' he says, 'and I'm *interested*!'

Or maybe you were THERE that day, I'm thinking. *And I will PROVE IT!*

'We could team up!' says Muscle, and his eyes gleam like diamonds. 'I could drive you round the sites of the heist in my car! You might remember something!'

As I stare back, I think: *I HATE him. But I so WANT to do what he's suggesting.*

'You're on,' I tell him.

CHAPTER NINE:
Stephen Maysmith, Police Detective

But *suddenly* there's loud BANGING on the front door.

'*Open up!*' calls a *mighty* voice, and I don't need to look out of the window to see who it is.

'It's the POLICE!' roars Stephen Maysmith.

'*Have you invited the police into my house?*' demands Muscle. 'If they even find that one snake, I could go to prison!'

'OPEN UP!'

roars Maysmith again.

'I can't *believe* you called the police to my house!' says Muscle.

'Don't worry!' says Cat. 'I'll deal with this.'

Muscle looks bothered.

'What will you say?' he asks.

'What *will* you say?' I ask, worried.

I definitely want to get Muscle arrested.
But I *don't* want it to happen before he
drives us round the scenes of the heist.

'Follow me and watch,' says Cat.
And she walks off down the stairs.

Muscle looks more bothered still, but he follows. I follow both of them with the mamba.

Through the frosted glass of the front door, I can see Stephen Maysmith. The rain is *lashing* down. He looks like a giant walrus flailing about out there. You can tell he is about to wield a big hammer to **SMASH** the door.

Don't you *dare* damage my property!
warns Muscle, snatching it open.

Maysmith sees Muscle. Maysmith sees
me. He sees I am holding a terrifying
snake.

'YOUNG MAN,' he says. 'Just *what*
are you doing with that snake? It looks
dangerous!'

'I am so glad you asked that,' says Cat.
'We found this snake in the bin outside!'

'What?' splutters Maysmith, looking at
me. 'Is this TRUE?'
'It is,' I tell him.

'And WHAT do you suggest a snake was doing in the bin?'

'I'd say he was resting,' I tell him.

'I opened the bin,' explains Cat, very coolly, 'since I wanted to throw away some rubbish. And then we saw the snake. So I texted you . . .'

Maysmith's getting *bamboozled* now.

'I know perfectly well this house belongs to a suspected felon, Jack "Muscle" Thompson,' he says. 'He is known to have owned Muscle's Pets, which had a number of exotic reptiles.'

'And because I had owned a snake *in the past*,' says Muscle, 'I was able to lend these nice children my snake-handling pole.'

He nods at me as if to say: *Isn't that how it was?*

'That's correct,' I tell the police officer. 'The snake is nothing to do with Mr Thompson. The snake was just hiding out in the bins – probably for a laugh.'

Stephen Maysmith loses it.

'*Do you expect me to believe,*' he says, '*this NONSENSE about the bins?*'

'Ask us *anything* about the bins,' I tell him. 'They're in there. The green one smells of cat sick. The black one smells of used nappy. Look. Look in there.'

Maysmith can't help himself. He opens the garage door. He sees bins.

'Do you have a warrant to search this house?' asks Cat.

'Of course!'

'I believe your warrant would have been to investigate some children in trouble,' smiles Cat. 'But we're actually *not* in trouble at all. So you can't search!'

'So you'll have to go!' Muscle tells him.

You can tell that Maysmith has been longing to nose around Muscle's house. He looks so furious he might EXPLODE (blasting custard creams all round the walls).

'DON'T MOVE!' he says. 'I will call
animal specialists IMMEDIATELY to come
and identify this snake! And I SHALL BE
WATCHING YOU!' he shouts to Muscle.

Furious, Maysmith bangs the door as he leaves.

Muscle grins.

'Nicely dealt with,' he says. 'So what do you suggest we do now?'

'I suggest,' says Cat, 'you take myself and Rory Branagan for a ride in your car to see if he remembers anything.'

'I'd be delighted,' says Muscle, 'but I suggest we leave quickly, and take that snake.'

'*We'll* hold on to him,' says Cat. 'In case you try anything.'

'Then you'd better take it in a tank,'
says Muscle.

CHAPTER TEN:
Casing the Joint

Five minutes later we are all in the car –
Muscle in the front, us in the back, the
guinea pigs still in the boot.

The black mamba is in his tank between me and Cat, but he's as good as gold. He's settled down for a snooze.

As we pull out into Niall Horan Drive, rain hammers against the canvas roof of the jeep.

Five minutes later, we are parked in the town centre. A man comes out of McAlister's Jeweller's, and the wind is so strong it smacks the door shut with a BANG.

Cat has the newspaper on her lap.

'So,' she says, 'the three masked men parked here.'

'The police say the bad guys went to the basement of Muscle's Pets,' says Cat, 'and let off an explosion that went through the wall . . .'

'They went into McAlister's Jeweller's, where they found Mr McAlister working on the Dame Norton Diamond.'

'They hit him, and took several diamonds, including the Dame Norton.'

'So why *didn't* they leave straight away?'
I ask her.

Cat shows me a diagram in the paper.
'The jeweller was working in a safe
room with a triple-locked door. The only
way out was back through the hole in the

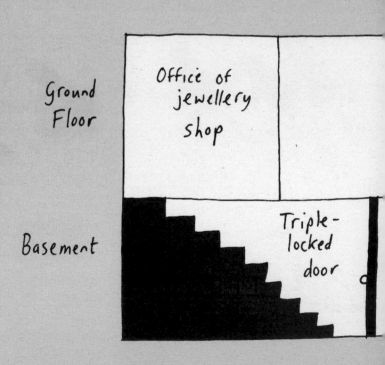

basement. Something BAD was blocking
the way.'

'Like what?'

'It's obvious!' says Cat.

'WHAT?'

'It was a snake,' says Cat. 'And not just *any* snake – the black mamba.'

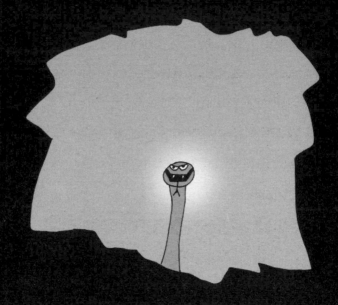

'*Where* would a black mamba have come from?' asks Muscle.

'There had just been an explosion under the pet shop. We *know* animals escaped. Rory ended up with a kitten.'

Muscle's eyes bulge.

'So how would the bad men escape,' he says, 'with a snake blocking the hole?'

'Maybe they called their getaway driver first, but he ran off. So they then called Padder Branagan,' says Cat. 'He was World Rally Champion – just the guy you'd want if you needed someone *quick* and *cool.*'

'I'm guessing he approached the snake from behind, while it was focused on the three men,' says Cat.

'He grabbed it by the neck. He passed it to the person who could handle it, which would have been YOU, Muscle.'

'I'm guessing you took it with you in your bag.'

Muscle says *nothing*, but his eyes gleam shiftily. *I am so SURE he's GUILTY!*

'I'm guessing Mr Bear took the Dame
Norton diamond in his bag,' says Cat.
'Who *was* the bear?' I ask.

'I don't know!' says Cat, but she carries
on with her theory . . .

'Outside,' she says, 'there were forty police officers approaching the town centre.'

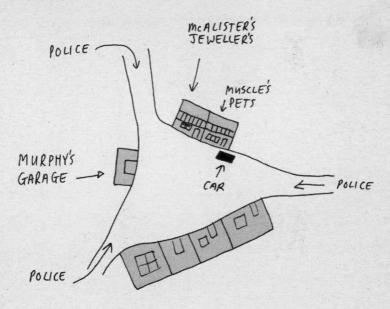

'Arriving there,' says Cat, pointing, 'police cars. There, police bikes. Arriving from behind, ten officers and two police horses. *So how the heck did the car escape?*'

'Because,' I answer, 'it was being driven by my dad, the greatest *genius* who ever sat behind a wheel!'

'*So how did he escape?*' asks Cat.

'He drove the car to the only possible escape route,' I say, and I point. '*Murphy's Garage*. He went up a ramp – the one you can see now.'

'And what then?'

'Then he flew the car out of the window,' I say, 'and over a wall!'

'Do you remember this?' asks Cat.
'No!'

'So are you just imagining it?'

'I don't know!'

'How can you *NOT* remember a flying car?'

'I was just looking after the kitten! I didn't want him to be scared!'

Muscle smiles.

'And I don't propose to take the same route now,' he says, 'but I'll drive you to the spot where your dad left the car.'

I give him a long, hard *detectivey* look.

'You need to stop on the way,' I tell him, 'at the yard of the old Anderson factory ...'

And as Muscle looks back at me, his eyes are cold and dead, like a fish on a slab.

'You got a problem with that?' I ask.
Furious, he says, *'No!'*

CHAPTER ELEVEN:
Into the Old Yard

We're there eight minutes later.

'This is where O'Gatiss's body was found. We parked here that day, didn't we?' I ask Muscle.

He gives me an EVIL look.

'How would I know?' he says.

'But it doesn't make sense,' Cat says. 'If you *had* just robbed a jeweller's, and there were police swarming everywhere, *why* would you stop?'

'To let men go,' I say. 'Also to change cars. We *know* that happened. In Maysmith's picture, I'm in a chunky old banger. Dad drove a cool sports car.'

Cat looks at me.

'Do you *remember* this?' she asks.

I look around the yard, and suddenly I *do* remember seeing the cool sports car. The door was open. A small cat was looking at me.

'Oh my God!' I say. 'I am *sure* of it! We changed cars, fast.'

'In the new car I didn't have the kitten! And *the bear* was now sitting beside me! He had a bag of his stuff. I remember thinking: *He's got his stuff, why can't I have my kitten?'*

Cat is looking at me very carefully.

'So the two that were left behind,' she says, 'were Mark "The Genius" O'Gatiss – and HIM!'

She points at Muscle.

'And I'd say that's *when you killed him!*'

'*Why* would I have killed him?' asks
Muscle quietly. 'And HOW?'

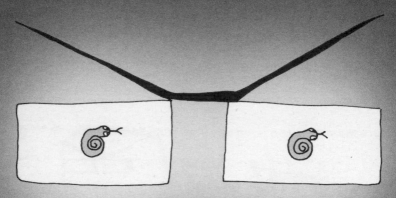

'You fought to get his diamonds from
him. Then you grabbed the mamba by the
neck, and jabbed him with it!'

'HOW ARE YOU INTENDING TO PROVE THAT?'

snarls Muscle.

'A black mamba is the only snake that leaves *dendrotoxins* and *three-finger toxins*,' says Cat.

'YOU own a mamba! The break-in happened under YOUR shop! YOU jabbed the Genius with the snake.'

Muscle says nothing.

Cat looks at me.

'Rory, come on – do you *remember* this guy?'

I think . . . but I don't remember Muscle on that day. But I *do* remember Mr Sheep. And . . .

'Hang on!' I say. 'We know the police found a bookmark on the floor!'

'So?' says Muscle.

'That *wasn't* a bookmark! It was a *tassel from a loafer*!' I say.

And I see O'Gatiss in my head one last time. His eyes *were* wild. And I know why – he'd just seen a snake. He was SCARED.

'I *know* you did it,' I tell Muscle.

But Muscle doesn't want to *discuss* any of this. As he zooms the car out of the yard, the wheels skid on the mud.

'Maybe it was the other man who killed the Genius!' says Muscle. '*Mr Bear!*'

'Michael Mulligan, you mean!' I say.
Cat turns sharply.

'*What?!* What makes you think it was
Michael Mulligan?'

'We know Mulligan knew Dad. He
bought a car festival from him. And
Mulligan is a DANGEROUS man. I'd
say Dad felt he *had* to agree when he was
asked to join the heist.'

'*Stop the car!*' says Cat.

Muscle stops.

'I *don't* believe Michael Mulligan was in
the car with you!' says Cat.

'Why not?' says Muscle.

'We know the police stopped that car,' says Cat, 'at a roadblock around the corner. You've seen the picture of yourself sitting with the starry blanket on your lap, Rory . . . There was no sign of Michael Mulligan in that picture!'

'But it was hot that day,' I say. '*Why would I have a blanket?*'

'I don't know!' says Cat.

'*Was Michael Mulligan under it??!!*'

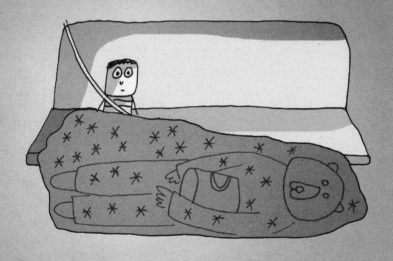

'But how would Stephen Maysmith *not* have found Michael Mulligan?' says Cat.

'Because that man is so stupid,' says Muscle, 'he would arrest his own foot!'

And as I look out at the road now, I can *remember* the police block. I can remember Stephen Maysmith.

(He was much thinner then! To picture him correctly, I have to suck seven years' worth of custard creams out of him!)

I remember Dad *talking* to him. I think Maysmith looked in the back of the car. But if Michael Mulligan was under the blanket, *why was he not seen*?

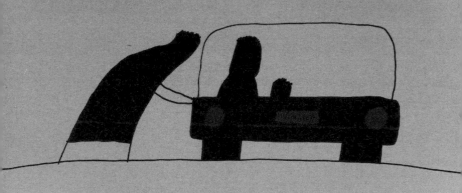

I know the memory is inside me somewhere . . . Suddenly I am feeling so *confused* and SO SICK.

That's it! I've got it!

'I REMEMBER IT!' I say. 'I *remember* what happened!'

'What?'

'I *puked*,' I announce, *'all over Stephen Maysmith's face!'*

'But *why* would you have done that?' says Cat.

'I had just eaten a double-chocolate ice cream, and then been driven so fast that we flew, so I *puked*, and Maysmith got it full in the face!'

I remember this now.

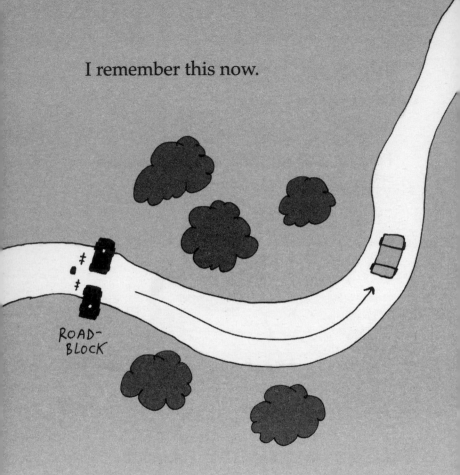

ROAD-
BLOCK

Maysmith told us to go. The car *zoomed* off. It had disappeared round the corner when the bear roared, *'For God's sake, Branagan – STOP!'*

Then he rose from the floor like an evil pukey monster rising from the swamp.

He pushed the blanket off him. He pulled open his bag. He wiped himself with some clothes.

'Turn the corner,' I tell Muscle now.

He does. We go round a bend. There are trees to the right.

'And this is where Michael Mulligan got out!' I announce.

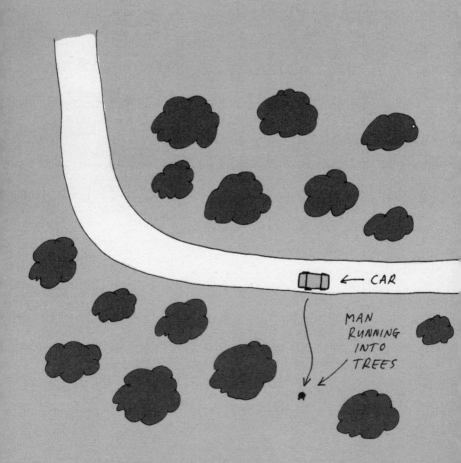

'How do you *know*?' says Cat. 'Did he take off the mask?'

'*No! He didn't!*'

'So how do you *know* it was Mulligan?' asks Cat.

'That's *why* he was at my house today: he didn't want to give me chocolate! He wanted to FIND OUT what I KNOW!'

'DID YOU SEE HIS FACE?!' says Cat.
'No!' I say. 'But I remember him
running off into the woods! He was
HUGE like Mulligan! It was HIM!'

Cat says nothing.

'The bear was Michael Mulligan,' I tell her. 'I *know* it.'

'And I'm going to take him DOWN!'

'But who *cares* about all that?' says Muscle. 'The only thing that matters is: ***which way did your dad run off?***'

I say nothing.

He drives the car round another corner.

We stop. We're now outside the old church. With a chill inside, I realise . . .

This is where we stopped that day! THIS is where Dad ran off! We're HERE.

CHAPTER TWELVE:
Outside the Old Church

'This is where you were found,' says Muscle, giving me a nasty look. '*Which way did your dad go?*'

'*I don't know!*' I tell him.

And I do not want to tell Muscle
anything, but I am definitely trying to
remember.

I look at the church to my right.

There is a dead tree outside, pointing at the sky and looking like the hand of a bony witch. The wind is howling around the building, and the ivy is shaking *furiously*.

In front of us, the rain is beating down so hard the whole windscreen looks underwater. Muscle turns on his wipers.

Then along the rain-lashed road comes a big black car.

Even from here I can see the two men inside are wearing top hats.

It's Mulligan's men – Derek 'Dent-head' O'Malley and Guy 'The Eyes' Murphy.

How do they even know we are here? The car stops in front of us. It's SO freaky . . .

Dent-head gets out. He doesn't care
about the evil rain. Even more freakily,
he's just looking at us.

It's all coming back. When we were here
seven years ago, there were *police* coming
from that direction.

Then, as the car cruises slowly by in the rain, it looks like a big evil shark. Eyes Murphy looks straight at us.

WHAT do they want with us?

I have an *awful* feeling about this. Eyes parks behind us.

And, oh my God, I know it!

It's just like it was for Dad that day. There were police ahead. There were police behind, and he had to escape. **Which way would he go?**

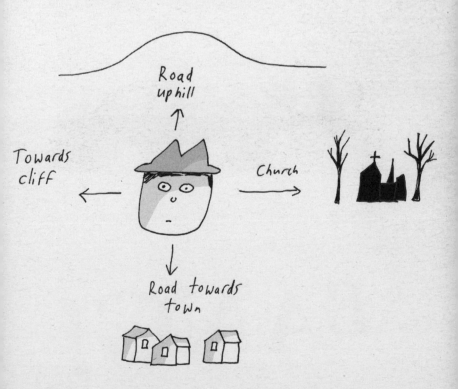

To my right, the wind is TEARING around the dead tree. It's a bony accusing finger *shaking* in the sky!

Suddenly something *soars* from it – the big wet nest of a crow.

BANG!

It *splats* against my window. I can see the big blue beady eyes of some baby crows.

I have never known the wind so bad that nests were being blown from trees! I want to run off.

I look left, to the other side of the road.
There's a wet path going between houses.

I realise: *That's IT!* That is the way DAD
would have wanted to go!

But DID he? *IS that what happened?*

Behind us Eyes has now got out of the car. Both he and Dent-head are walking towards us.

'Gordon Bennett,' says Muscle. 'What do they want?'

He gets out of the car. Cat gets out too.

'Don't leave me,' I tell them. I want to follow.

Suddenly Muscle snaps. He opens my door.

'I am not *SURPRISED your dad ran off and left you!*' he snarls. '*You are so ANNOYING! Will you just SIT THERE and REMEMBER* **WHICH WAY** *HE WENT!*'

And for a second I am hit by thoughts so
EVIL, they're like snarling *vampire* bats . . .

Did Dad go because I was so annoying?

Is it all   MY FAULT?

But then I think of Dad in the park. I think of him teaching me to swim. I know he loved me!

I'm thinking: *SO WHY DID HE GO?* And then . . .

I *REMEMBER* it.

Dad got out. He opened my door. He looked at me. But then he noticed *something* on the floor. He paused. He looked *so* surprised.

He bent down. He picked it up. I couldn't see what it was. His face was all pale. He stared.

Then suddenly his face sparkled like magic, and I know why . . .

The sun was shining and Dad was holding the Dame Norton Diamond!

Michael Mulligan must have accidentally pulled it from his bag as he reached for something to wipe himself. It must have dropped to the floor. I remember . . .

Dad looked at me. His face was white.

He looked to the churchyard on his left.

I look there now.

But then something absolutely
TERRIBLE happens . . .

I hear a loud

CRACK.

And the bony old tree comes
PLUNGING down towards me.

It cuts straight through the canvas
roof of the car. It SMASHES the
window to my left.

It falls,

BANG,

hitting the door.

A branch is pinning my legs, but the tree's hardly touched me. *Luck is on my side! A dead tree has fallen, and it's completely MISSED me . . .*

. . . but it has *SMASHED* the tank of the black mamba!

CHAPTER THIRTEEN:
Dead

And, fair enough, I can actually see it from the mamba's point of view. He was sleeping, and he's been woken up.

My brother once woke me up by leaping on my bed and letting off a klaxon by my head.

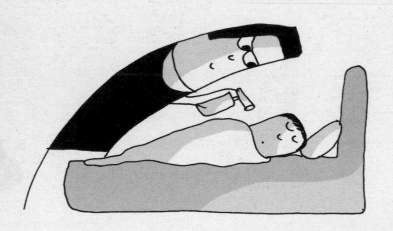

Oh my God, I fairly SPRANG from the bed like a salmon and HEADBUTTED my brother!

And it's like that for the snake now.

He was fast asleep – probably dreaming happy snaky dreams, in which he was on holiday with other black mambas – Mrs Mamba, Baby Mamba and all the auntie Mambas.

Suddenly he is SMACKED AWAKE.
And he is like anyone who is angry – he
wants someone to blame.

If my brother was here, he'd probably
headbutt him. But the only person is me.
So he does it.

The snake bites me.

Once,

twice,

three times, fast, on my arm.

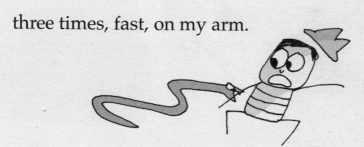

Right away I go very still. I get a taste
like wet metal in my mouth. I can't move.
I can't swallow. I can't breathe. I can't *see*.
And then suddenly it's very strange . . .

I feel I am looking down on the car from above. I can see the tree. I can see everyone standing around looking surprised.

Cat

Guy 'The Eyes' Murphy

Derek 'Dent-head' O'Malley

Tree stump

Jack 'Muscle'
Thompson

Then suddenly everything is sunny. My life is *flashing* before me . . .

I see Dad pushing me on a swing.

I see Dad telling stories by a campfire.

And then I am seeing Dad running off
that day. He heads across the road and
down the path!

I am seeing Dad when he was still with us. We are on a beach and we're having such a good time. I am digging an enormous hole. My mum is smiling from a deck chair.

My brother is being chased by a crab.
But my dad is *laughing,* and suddenly I
know it. *This is where he was happiest – when
he was with us and we were all on holiday!*

And then it's very strange. I feel I am coming up from a hole to another beach, and it is *amazing*. I see the sea *sparkling*. I see the biggest, best treehouse of all time. I see *dogs* flying about.

I'm thinking: *This isn't happening!* Then . . .

Oh my God, I'm dying!

I see my mum at home.

Somehow she knows I'm dying, and she's so sad.

I see Mrs Welkin and Wilkins. They know too, and they are even more sad – especially Wilkins.

And I am really sad. I realise I will never hug that dog again!

I see Cat. I see every freckle on her face, and I can't BELIEVE I'll never solve crimes with her again. She is the best friend I've ever had!

I am *soooooo* sad. And then, suddenly . . .

OWWWWW!

I get a *savage* pain in my right arm. I feel I am being dragged down through a tunnel.

I am back in the car, and I see Cat.
She has jabbed me in the arm with the
snakebite antivenom.

She is tying Muscle's cravat round
my arm.

'Are you OK?' she asks, very worried.

And I actually am. I feel a bit groggy. I
also feel I could fight a tiger.

'Never better!' I say. And I quickly
wriggle out from under the tree and escape
the car.

'What are you DOING?' asks Cat.

And I say the words I was BORN to say.

'Come on!' I command. 'We have a
CASE to CRACK!'

And I *run*!

CHAPTER FOURTEEN:
High-speed Detective Action

I can't be stopped. I am running across the road.

I run down the path, just the way Dad did that day.

Muscle is following.

As I reach the end of the path, I see that it comes out at the road that goes along the top of the cliff. The storm has passed.

Suddenly the sky lights up. I can see the

sea gleaming at the bottom of the cliff.
I look down. I know that along the coast
is . . . *Ballycove.*

*THAT'S where we went for our holidays –
the best holidays EVER!*

On the other side of the road, I see a bus stop. I already know where the bus goes: *Ballycove. That's where Dad will be HIDING!*

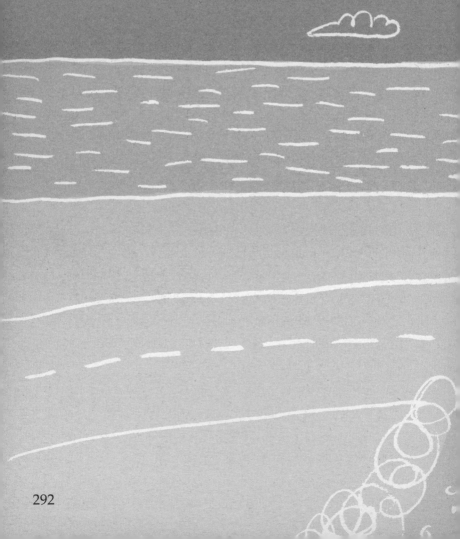

I'm guessing he ran to a bus and got on.
But there's no bus now.

There's a police car.

Stephen Maysmith gets out of it. And
THAT is what starts the ACTION.

Maysmith sees me running. He sees
Muscle behind me.

'JACK "MUSCLE"
THOMPSON,'

he roars. 'I told you I was sending the
animal experts. STOP!'

But Muscle doesn't want to stop.
He turns and sprints back towards the
church.

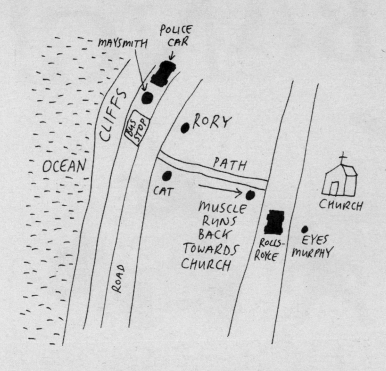

'*Stop him!*' I shout to Cat. But Muscle
runs right by her. He's away. He's making
his way to the top of the path.

But then Dent-head drives forward . . .

BANG!

Muscle somersaults over the bonnet.
But then he's up. He's running. But we're
after him . . .

. . . and Cat and I bring him down – one on each leg.

'What are you doing?' he says furiously.

'We are arresting you,' Cat tells him,
'for the murder of Mark O'Gatiss.'

By now, Stephen Maysmith is with us.

'What are you two talking about?' he
says.

'He killed the Genius!' I say.

'We didn't tell you the truth before,' says Cat. 'That snake at his house BELONGS TO HIM! And it's a **BLACK MAMBA**, the ONLY snake that produces the toxins that killed O'Gatiss! He keeps it in a *secret room* in his house!'

'The tassel you found at the crime scene was from *his shoe*,' I tell Maysmith. 'And if you look in that car, you'll find the snake! So you *have* evidence! You have a murder weapon! And you have a killer. ***HIM!***'

Muscle knows we've got him. He tries to RUN.

And that's when Stephen Maysmith PUNCHES his lights out.

Then he whips out the cuffs.

CHAPTER FIFTEEN:
My Brother

After that things go fast. Stephen
Maysmith has already called for back-up,
so more police are here in no time at all.

They take Muscle away in a big van. An expert arrives and removes the snake. I'm actually sad to see the long feller go.

Eyes and Dent-head scarper. I am still wondering how come they turned up, but I'm now more bothered about the guinea pigs. I tell Maysmith and we take them out of Muscle's jeep and load them into the police car.

Then Maysmith takes us home in it –
which of course we always LOVE.

'We've been trying to nail Muscle for
seven years,' says Stephen Maysmith.

'You should have asked for our help
before!' I tell him.

'But you're kids!'

'And sometimes kids see things grown-ups miss!'

'Fair enough,' says Maysmith. 'I don't know how to thank you.'

'Just . . . stop here,' I tell him.

We're outside Corner Boy's. We take the boxes to his door and knock. Corner Boy opens it.

'We have a delivery for you!' I tell him.

Corner Boy opens a box. Then he gasps. And the guinea pigs think they're seeing the Lord of All Guinea Pigs. A big *chorus* of them all SQUEAK SQUEAK SQUEAK in return.

Corner Boy takes out his favourite ones –
Mike Tyson and his baby.

'*Mike Tyson!*' squeals Corner Boy.

And he's so happy, he starts crying.

'RORY and CAT!' he says. 'THANK
YOU! *You are the GREATEST
DETECTIVES there will ever be!*'

And I'm happy to hear it. But I'm not
hanging about to talk about it. We head
home.

As Cat reaches her front door, I stop her.

'I should thank you,' I say to her. 'You did just save my life!'

'*Deadly* Branagan,' she says. 'I can't let you go. I've not finished with you yet!'

'Cat,' I say, 'when the snake bit me . . . I cracked it.'

'What?'

'I *know* where Dad went!'

'WHERE?'

'I'll TAKE you,' I tell her. 'Tomorrow.'

She just stares.

'And, Cat?'

'What?'

'When the snake bit me. For a moment, I thought I'd died.'

'Did you?'

'Yes . . . I saw an enormous treehouse. And there were sausage dogs, flying.'

She smiles, but you can tell she doesn't
believe me.

'But Rory . . .' she whispers. 'Did you
really see that? Or did you just *imagine* it?'

'I don't care,' I say. 'I saw it. And when
I get to heaven, I know there'll be sausage
dogs!'

'You're such an *eejit*,' she breathes, 'but that's why we *love* you!'

She touches her hand to my cheek. Then she goes into her house.

I go into mine.

And this is what *annoys* me . . . I have *literally* JUST opened the door and my brother shouts:

'DON'T LET THAT DOOR SLAM!'

So I slam it – **BANG**

– just to *annoy* him.

Immediately he comes *springing* out of
the kitchen with his hummus.

'*WHERE* have you been?' he asks.
'I have been *detectiving* and solving
crimes,' I tell him, 'and I have found out
where Dad went!'

'No, you *haven't*,' he sneers. 'You have been out being a LOSER!'

And then, just to be *evil*, he takes some hummus, and he smears it on my face.

Well, I am a detective, like Hercule Poirot or Sherlock Holmes, and I'll not stand by while people *smear hummus on my face*!

'I *know* where he went!' I say again. 'And I will PROVE it tomorrow!'

And I take his stupid hummus pot and I *splat it on his head.*

SQUELCH!

For a second, the pot stops there, looking like a tiny bowler hat.

'I will *get you!*' shouts my brother.

But I don't care about him. I just dodge
past, and head up to my room.

Where I find, to my
surprise, I've got a
visitor . . .

It's Wilkins Welkin. Curled up sleepily on the bed, he gently wags his tail.

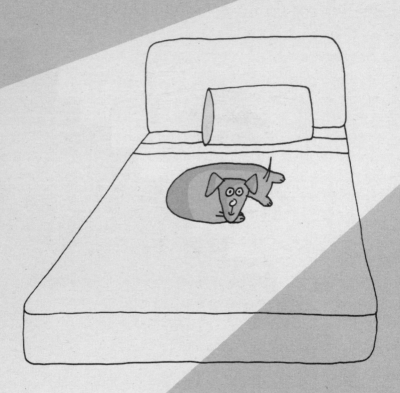

I lie down next to him. I'm suddenly feeling all *groggy* and *spaced out* now, but very *glad* to see him.

'Why wouldn't sausage dogs go to heaven?' I whisper. 'If they didn't, their people would miss them too much!'

Wilkins agrees. Well . . . he farts gently and shows me his belly. I give him a tickle.

Outside I can feel the big wide
world getting dark. I know we solved
a crime today. And, even better, I know
somewhere in Ballycove my dad is
waiting.

I don't know WHERE in Ballycove he
is, but I KNOW I'll find him.

Because I am Rory Branagan, and I may not be the greatest detective there'll ever be.

But I'm most definitely a detective.

The End

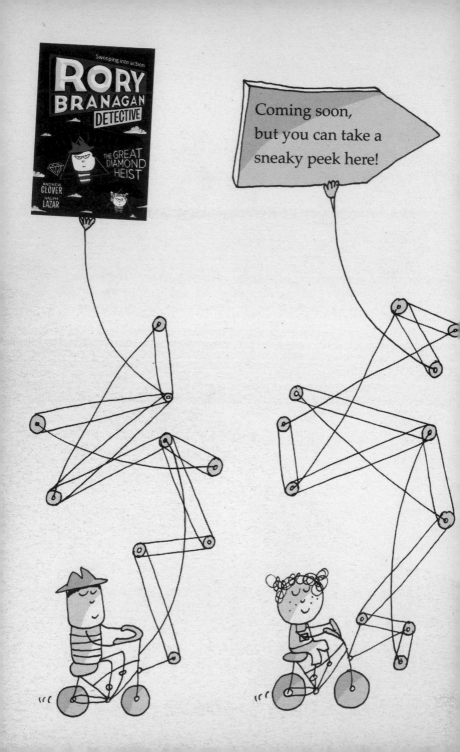

We reach Granny Gilligan's house – a bungalow at the edge of Ballycove.

'You're *welcome* to come in!' says Mrs Welkin.

'Sorry, we have detective work to do,'
I tell her. (*I can't believe it! We're finding
Dad!*)

'Let me give you something!' says Mrs
Welkin.

'*What?*' I ask.

'It's a tuna sandwich.'

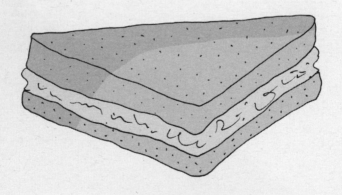

I'm thinking if **bad guys** appear, we'll
need more than a tuna sandwich.

Wilkins Welkin wants to help too. He drops a manky old ball at my feet.

I say, 'Thank you, my friend!' and put it in my pocket.

'And *I* will lend you the *Master Blaster*!'
says Corner Boy.

Already, I am tensing up. Corner Boy
won't STOP going on about his go-kart,
called the Master Blaster.

'You HAVE to see what I've done to it!'
he says.

'That's OK,' I tell him, but it's NO USE.
In seconds, he's showing it to us.

It looks like an alien spaceship – if the
aliens were EEJITS, who made spaceships
by dropping wood into glue.

'The latest addition,' he tells me, 'is this
HONKER!' He squeezes it.

HONK, HONK.

'And,' he continues, 'I added the GUNK GUN!' He shows me a spray bottle. 'I filled it with pondwater,' he says proudly, 'but I added cat poo!'

'It's very kind of you,' says Cat. 'But just say the Master Blaster was *damaged* – how would you feel then?'

'Then I would be very PROUD,' says Corner Boy, 'that it was damaged on an *investigation*! You two are my best friends! You're the ones who called me Special Agent Corner Boy!'

'We'll take it,' says Cat. 'Thank you, Corner Boy.'

'Special *Agent* Corner Boy!' says Corner Boy.

'Special *Agent* Corner Boy,' says Cat.

But just then, the black Rolls-Royce goes by.

It's Dent-head O'Malley and Eyes Murphy! TERRIFIED, Cat and I dive behind the fence.

We wait for them to clear off, and then we go ourselves – with the Master Blaster.

But we quickly find that while it has a HONKER, a GUNK GUN and a Frisbee steering wheel . . . it *doesn't* actually have BRAKES.

Soon we're bombing down the road like a TRAIN . . .

... And we're about to CRASH –
SMASH!! – into the harbour wall.

To be continued . . .

**Read more inside
the final book of
the series!**

Swooping down to stamp out crime

RORY BRANAGAN
DETECTIVE

THE GREAT
DIAMOND
HEIST

ANDREW
CLOVER

RALPH
LAZAR

Coming
soon!

Discover where Rory's adventures began . . .

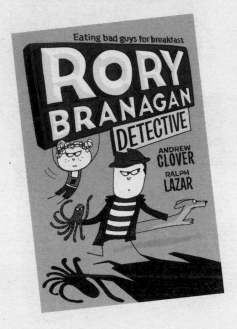

People always say: 'How do you become a detective?' and I say: 'Ahhh, you don't just suddenly find yourself *sneaking* up on baddies, or *chasing* them, or *fighting them*, or living a life of constant deadly danger – you have to WANT it. So why did *I* want it? I just wanted to find my dad. And I will – but first I have to track down some POISONERS!

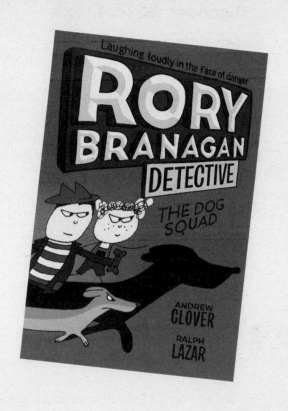

I, Rory Branagan, have uncovered a crime *right where I live*. Some *flip-flaps* are STEALING dogs. I am going to work out *who* they are and I am going to *stop* them, because I love *all* dogs. But the dog I love most, by about a *million miles*, is Wilkins Welkin, and he is in DANGER.

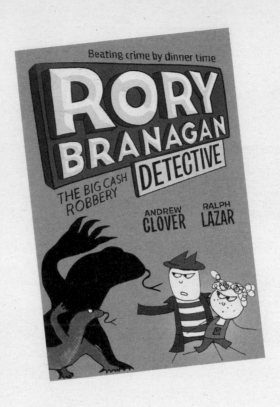

This week we had the biggest, *best* school fete
of all time. We had *bouncy castles, sumo wrestling*
and a real live *Komodo dragon*. We earned *loads* of
money, but then some evil *thief* stole it! So it's up
to me to find out *who* – and nobody will stop me,
not even a DRAGON!

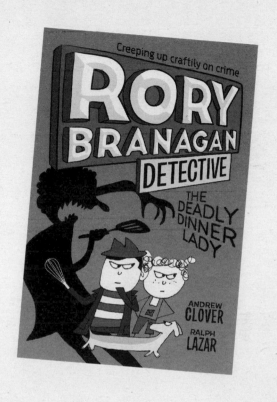

My school is having a talent show – with Mr
Bolton's *ridiculous* rap, Mr Meeton's *epic* guitar
solos and my friend Cat's amazing dance – but,
right in the middle of it, there is the DEADLIEST
crime in the history of our school. I have to find
out *who* did it and *why* – before they strike again!

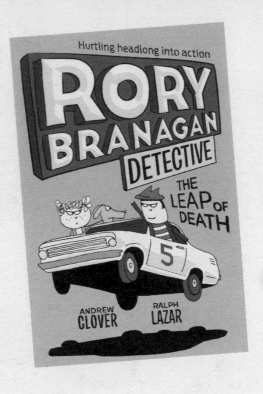

I'm at a stunt festival called Car Bonanza and it is
EPIC. People are *driving down cliffs*, leaping over
tanks filled with *crocodiles* and *jumping* out of
planes! But then – DISASTER – someone *messes*
with a car and the stuntman CRASHES. *Who* tried
to kill him? I must find out QUICK!